The Middle Toe of the Right Foot

*A Macabre Tale of Dueling Spirits
and Sinister Hauntings*

A Modern Translation

Adapted for the Contemporary Reader

Ambrose Bierce

Translated by Tim Zengerink

Table of Contents

Preface - Message to the Reader

What If You Could Help Rebuild the Greatest Library in Human History?

Thousands of years ago, the Library of Alexandria stood as the crown jewel of human achievement — a sanctuary where the collected wisdom of every known civilization was gathered, preserved, and shared freely.

And then, it was lost.

Through fire, conquest, and the slow erosion of time, humanity lost not just books — but ideas, dreams, discoveries, and stories that could have changed the world forever.

Today, the Library of Alexandria lives again — and you are invited to be a part of its restoration.

Our mission is simple yet profound:

To rebuild the greatest library the world has ever known, and to translate all timeless works into every language and dialect, so that no seeker of knowledge is ever left behind again.

By joining our movement to rebuild the modern Library of Alexandria, you become part of an unprecedented mission:

- **Unlimited Access to the Greatest Audiobooks & eBooks Ever Written:**

  Instantly explore thousands of legendary works—Plato, Shakespeare, Jane Austen, Leo Tolstoy, and countless more. All instantly available to read or listen, placing a complete literary universe at your fingertips.

- **Beautiful Paperback & Deluxe Editions at Printing Cost**

  Own any title as an elegant paperback, deluxe hardcover, or stunning collectible boxset—offered to you at true printing cost, delivered straight to your door. Build your personal Library of Alexandria, crafted for beauty, built for durability, and worthy of proud display.

- **Fresh Translations for Modern Readers—in Every Language & Dialect**

  Enjoy timeless masterpieces reimagined in clear, contemporary language—no more outdated phrases or obscure references. Alongside the original versions, we're tirelessly translating these classics into every language and dialect imaginable, ensuring accessibility and understanding across cultures and generations.

- **Join a Global Renaissance of Literature & Knowledge**

  You directly support expanding our library, publishing deluxe editions at true cost, translating works into all global languages, and bringing humanity's greatest stories to people everywhere. By joining today, you're not just preserving a legacy of masterpieces; you set in motion a powerful wave of literary accessibility.

Become a Torchbearer of Knowledge.

Join us for free now at **LibraryofAlexandria.com**

Together, we will ensure that the light of human wisdom never fades again.

With gratitude and a shared love of knowledge,

The Modern Library of Alexandria Team

Visit:

www.libraryofalexandria.com

Or scan the code below:

Introduction

Sinister Justice, Haunted Conscience, and the American Gothic

Ambrose Bierce's The Middle Toe of the Right Foot, first published in the late 19th century, is a quintessential example of the American gothic: a tale that weds supernatural horror with moral reckoning, set against the backdrop of a land as wild and unforgiving as the past it conceals. Bierce, often called the "wickedest man in San Francisco" and best remembered for his sardonic wit and military-inflected horror, here delivers a compact ghost story whose brevity only enhances its lingering dread. As with much of Bierce's fiction, the tale unfolds like a fable, with a precise and merciless sense of justice that leaves no room for redemption.

At the heart of the story is an unnamed man who arrives in the fictional town of Hurlyburly, Texas. There he becomes embroiled in a local legend about a haunted house—a structure abandoned for years after a gruesome and mysterious murder. In an act of bravado and calculated malice, the man agrees to a contest: he and another local will enter the house and remain in separate darkened rooms, unarmed, until dawn. As the night unfolds, however, we learn the man's true identity—he is the murderer who once lived in that house, the killer of a wife and children now returned to the scene of his crime. The haunting that follows is not just supernatural. It is retributive. He is judged, not in a courtroom, but by a force that transcends law.

The Middle Toe of the Right Foot is not merely a ghost story. It is an indictment of repression, a meditation on guilt, and a narrative weapon sharpened by Bierce's own experiences in war, politics, and personal tragedy. The title itself—strange, grotesque, almost absurd—hints at a narrative style that blends psychological horror with grotesque irony. As Bierce so often did, he confronts us with the uncomfortable truth that evil is not buried by time, and that justice may take the form of silence, darkness, and the severed remnants of what once passed for humanity.

In this introduction, we will explore the story's function as a gothic parable, its historical and cultural underpinnings, and its unique place in Bierce's broader literary output. We will see how The Middle Toe of the Right Foot turns domestic violence into ghostly retribution, how it leverages regional folklore for psychological horror, and how it remains a cutting, unforgettable tale more than a century after it was written.

The Haunted House as Courtroom: Supernatural Vengeance and Moral Order

The core of Bierce's story is deceptively simple: a man is lured back to the house where he committed a triple murder and forced to face something—or someone—in the dark. But this simplicity masks a carefully constructed framework of gothic tropes reimagined with an American sensibility. The haunted house here is not merely a backdrop. It is the instrument of justice. Its walls do not echo with fear—they enforce it.

Bierce was not interested in ghosts as mere phantoms. He used the supernatural as a literary scalpel, carving through layers of moral decay. In this story, the ghost is not a wailing spirit seeking mercy. It is a quiet, invisible presence that delivers judgment without explanation. The house does not scream. It does not shake. It simply isolates the guilty and watches him unravel.

The silence of the house is key. Gothic literature traditionally relies on dramatic confrontation—apparitions, curses, exorcisms. Bierce offers none of this. The horror in The Middle Toe of the Right Foot lies in waiting, in uncertainty, in the unbearable pressure of memory unburied. The man knows the house. He recognizes the walls. He senses what he has returned to, even before the reader does. The supernatural does not announce itself. It emerges as if it were always there.

This subtlety makes the story resonate beyond its ghostly premise. It becomes a study in conscience. The protagonist may be a killer, but he is also human. He tries to dismiss the past, to hide behind anonymity, to rely on bravado. But none of this matters once he steps into the house. There, the old rules no longer apply. Time folds inward. Identity returns. Guilt becomes manifest.

The "middle toe" of the title—severed, buried, discovered—serves as the grotesque clue that confirms the killer's identity. It is a literal piece of the past, a marker of truth that survives long after lies have faded. In this, Bierce echoes Poe's obsession with buried evidence and retributive fate. But unlike Poe, Bierce adds a modern coldness. There is no madness, no poetry, no plea. Only exposure.

Bierce and the American Gothic: Violence, War, and the Moral Frontier

Ambrose Bierce's literary style was shaped by violence—personal, political, and national. As a Civil War veteran, he witnessed firsthand the brutality of battle. As a journalist, he was a relentless critic of hypocrisy and corruption. And as a fiction writer, he wielded irony like a sword. In The Middle Toe of the Right Foot, all of these influences converge.

American gothic fiction, as distinct from its European counterpart, often locates horror not in crumbling castles or decaying aristocracies, but in the frontier, the wilderness, and the haunted house. These are spaces where the veneer of civilization thins, and the individual is exposed to forces—natural, historical, or spiritual—beyond control. Bierce harnesses this tradition with ruthless precision. His Hurlyburly is not a supernatural realm. It is a real town filled with real people, whose folklore conceals a truth far more terrifying than rumor.

Bierce also understood the psychological impact of suppressed violence. His characters rarely express guilt in conventional terms. Instead, they are eaten alive by it, undone by silence, by time, by the weight of what they refuse to remember. The protagonist in The Middle Toe of the Right Foot is not pursued by mobs or police. He is pursued by something older and deeper: the inevitability of moral consequence.

In this, the story can be read as a uniquely American parable of manifest guilt. The man leaves, reinvents himself, and returns, believing the past is buried. But the land remembers. The house remembers. And the toe, grotesque as it is, becomes a relic of unforgotten sin. This theme of return—of the past refusing to stay buried—echoes throughout Bierce's fiction, most famously in An Occurrence at Owl Creek Bridge, where time itself warps in the face of death.

But where that story offers a dream of escape, The Middle Toe offers none. There is no mercy, no delusion. Only truth.

Legacy, Irony, and the Severed Remains of Redemption

The Middle Toe of the Right Foot is a masterclass in literary compression. In just a few pages, Bierce constructs a gothic narrative, reveals a murder mystery, critiques the failure of justice, and delivers supernatural vengeance. The story's title alone invites analysis: why such a strange and specific name? The answer lies in Bierce's genius for ironic focus. He draws the reader in with a title that sounds absurd, even humorous. But by the end, the toe is no joke. It is the key to everything.

This irony is Bierce's trademark. He did not believe in sentimentality. He distrusted systems of power. And he rarely allowed his characters the dignity of redemption. The protagonist is not given a chance to explain himself or to apologize. He is not even named until after his death. He is reduced to a body, a scream, and a memory that now belongs to the town he once tried to deceive.

What makes the story endure is its moral clarity. In a world where murder can be hidden, where names can be changed, and where society may forget, Bierce insists that something larger does not. Whether we call it fate, conscience, or ghostly justice, there is a force that waits. It may not speak. But it knows.

The final scene—the door flung open, the man found dead, the realization dawning among the townspeople—is not catharsis. It is revelation. And in that revelation is Bierce's ultimate message: that the past, once violated, does not rest.

More than a ghost story, The Middle Toe of the Right Foot is a gothic indictment of moral cowardice. It asks not whether ghosts are real, but whether guilt can be silenced. It answers: no. Not in this world, and not in the next.

Ambrose Bierce disappeared mysteriously in 1914, vanishing into Mexico and never returning. Some say he died in the revolution. Others claim he faked his death. Whatever the truth, his fiction remains. And stories like The Middle Toe of the Right Foot remind us that, in the gothic imagination, disappearance is never escape. It is only the beginning of the reckoning.

Chapter I

Everyone around here knows the old Manton house is haunted. People in the countryside nearby and even folks in the town of Marshall, just a mile away, believe it without question. The only ones who don't are the kind of people others might call "weird" once that word becomes common in the local newspaper, the Marshall Advance. There are two kinds of proof the house is haunted: the stories of people who claim they've seen things, and the house itself. Some may argue about the stories, but the condition of the house is something anyone can see for themselves.

To begin with, no one has lived there for over ten years. The house and its sheds are slowly falling apart, which is a pretty strong clue to most people. It's set a little off the quietest stretch of road between Marshall and Harriston, in what used to be a farm. Now it's just a field full of weeds, broken fences, and thorny bushes growing over rocky land that hasn't seen a plow in years. The house is still standing but is stained and worn from years of wind and rain. Most of the windows are broken or boarded up, thanks to local kids who throw rocks for fun. The house is two stories tall and almost square in shape. The front door sits between two windows that are covered up completely. The windows upstairs are open to the weather. Tall grass and thick weeds grow all around, and a few old trees, bent from storms, lean as if they're trying to escape. One writer for the Advance once joked, "Of course the Manton house is haunted—just look at it."

And if the creepy look wasn't enough, there's more. Ten years ago, Mr. Manton murdered his wife and two young children in the middle of the night and then disappeared without a trace. That terrible event convinced people that the house is filled with something dark.

One warm evening, four men arrived at the Manton house in a wagon. Three of them got out right away. The driver tied the horses to the last post still standing from an old fence. The fourth man stayed seated.

"Come on," one of the others said, walking up to him while the rest headed toward the house. "This is the place."

The man didn't move. "This is a trap," he said angrily. "And I think you're part of it."

"Maybe I am," the other man answered coolly, locking eyes with him. "But you agreed to let the other side pick the spot. Unless you're afraid of ghosts…"

"I'm not afraid of anything," the man growled, swearing as he jumped down.

They joined the others at the front door. One of them had already forced it open, though it took effort because the hinges and lock were rusted. Inside, it was pitch black. The man who had opened the door pulled out a candle and matches, lit it, and opened a door on the right. It led into a large, square room. The candle barely lit it. A thick layer of dust covered the floor, softening their footsteps. Cobwebs stretched from the ceiling and corners like old rags, swaying in the air. There were two windows, but both were boarded up from the outside. The room had no fireplace, no furniture—just cobwebs, dust, and the four men.

They looked strange in the yellow candlelight, especially the man who had refused to get out of the wagon. He was hard to ignore. He was middle-aged, tall, and powerfully built. He looked like someone who could do serious damage. He had no beard, short gray hair, and a forehead marked with deep lines. His thick black eyebrows almost met in the middle, and his deep-set eyes glowed faintly. His wide jaw and tight mouth made him look even scarier. His skin was so pale, he looked like all the blood had been drained from his body.

The other three looked normal—like anyone you might pass on the street and forget. They were all younger than the pale man, and one of them stood apart from him. It was clear they didn't get along. They didn't even look at each other.

"Gentlemen," said the man holding the candle and keys, "everything's ready. Are you ready, Mr. Rosser?"

Rosser, the man standing alone, nodded and gave a small smile.

"And you, Mr. Grossmith?"

The big man nodded too, but with a scowl.

"Please take off your outer clothes."

They removed their hats, jackets, vests, and ties, and tossed them outside into the hall. The man with the candle gave a signal, and the fourth man—the one who had convinced Grossmith to get out of the wagon—pulled two long, sharp knives from his coat. He took them out of their sheaths.

"They're identical," he said, handing one to each man—because by now, it was obvious: this was a duel.

Each man held his knife close to the candlelight, checking the blade and handle. They tested their strength by pushing them against their knees. Then, each was searched by the other's second to make sure no one had any hidden weapons.

"If that's alright with you, Mr. Grossmith," said the man with the candle, "please stand in that corner."

He pointed to the farthest side of the room. Grossmith walked there, and his second gave him a cold handshake. Rosser stood in the corner closest to the door. After whispering something to his second, that man also stepped away and stood by the door.

Suddenly, the candle went out. The room went completely dark. Maybe a breeze from the open door had blown it out, but whatever it was, it surprised them all.

"Gentlemen," said a voice—now strange and unfamiliar in the darkness—"don't move until you hear the front door close."

They heard footsteps, the inside door closing, and finally the front door slamming shut so hard it shook the whole house.

A few minutes later, a farmer's son was heading home when he saw a wagon racing toward Marshall. He swore he saw three figures on the front seat: two men sitting down, and a third standing behind them, gripping their shoulders. The two in front looked like they were trying to get away. The figure in back was dressed in white and had clearly jumped onto the wagon as it passed the haunted house. Since the boy had seen ghosts before, people believed him.

The next day, the Advance ran the story, adding some dramatic touches and offering the men involved a chance to share their side. But no one ever did.

Chapter II

The things that led to the "duel in the dark" were actually pretty simple. One evening, three young men from the town of Marshall were sitting on the porch of the local hotel, relaxing in a quiet corner. They were smoking and chatting about topics that educated Southern men their age usually found interesting. Their names were King, Sancher, and Rosser.

Not far from them, sitting alone but close enough to hear everything, was another man. He was a stranger. They only knew that he had arrived earlier that day by stagecoach and had signed the hotel guestbook with the name "Robert Grossmith." No one had seen him speak to anyone other than the hotel clerk. He kept to himself and seemed to prefer being alone—or, as a local newspaper reporter joked, he "liked the company of dark thoughts." But to be fair, that reporter was known for drinking too much and had been annoyed when Grossmith refused to give him an interview.

"I can't stand any kind of flaw in a woman," said King. "Whether she was born with it or it happened later. I believe that if someone has a physical problem, they probably have a mental or emotional problem too."

"So what you're saying," Rosser replied seriously, "is that a woman without a nose probably wouldn't have much of a chance with you."

"That's one way to put it," King answered. "But I really mean it. I once broke up with a lovely girl because I found out—by accident—that she was missing a toe. Maybe that was mean, but if I'd married her, we would've both been miserable."

Sancher laughed. "Well, because of your high standards, she married someone else—and he ended up cutting her throat."

"So you know who I'm talking about," said King. "Yeah, she married Manton. But I'm not sure he was very accepting either. Maybe he killed her when he found out she didn't have that all-important middle toe on her right foot."

"Look at that guy," Rosser said in a low voice, nodding toward the stranger.

Grossmith was clearly listening to everything.

"What nerve," King muttered. "What should we do?"

"That's simple," Rosser said, getting up. "Sir," he said to Grossmith, "I think it would be best if you moved your chair to the other side of the porch. You don't seem used to being around decent company."

Grossmith jumped up, fists clenched and face pale with anger. Now all four men were standing. Sancher quickly stepped between them.

"You're overreacting and being unfair," he told Rosser. "This man didn't do anything wrong."

But Rosser refused to take it back. And in those days, an insult like that usually meant a fight was coming.

"I expect the respect due to any gentleman," Grossmith said, now calmer. "I don't know anyone around here. Sir," he added, turning to Sancher, "would you be willing to act as my second?"

Sancher agreed, though he didn't feel great about it—there was something about Grossmith that made him uneasy. King, who hadn't spoken during the fight but had been watching Grossmith closely, nodded to show he would stand for Rosser. And with that, the challenge was accepted, and a duel was set for the following night.

You already know what kind of duel it was—two men with knives in total darkness. These kinds of brutal fights used to be more common in the American Southwest than they are now. But this one showed how little real honor there was beneath all the talk of "gentlemanly" behavior.

Chapter III

In the bright heat of a summer afternoon, the old Manton house didn't look scary at all. It seemed completely normal. The sunlight covered it gently, almost like it didn't care about the dark stories people told. The grass out front was green and full of life—not overgrown, just healthy. Even the weeds looked more like flowers than pests. The trees that once seemed broken and struggling now stood calmly, filled with light and the sounds of birds singing. The empty windows upstairs, with no glass, didn't look spooky either. The soft light pouring through them made them seem peaceful. Even the heat rising from the rocky fields added to the feeling that everything was warm and alive—not haunted.

That's how the house appeared to Sheriff Adams and the two men who came with him from the nearby town of Marshall. One of them was Mr. King, the sheriff's deputy. The other was Mr. Brewer, brother of the late Mrs. Manton. According to state law, since no one had lived on the property for a long time and no one knew where the owner had gone, the sheriff was in charge of it. Brewer had gone to court, trying to claim the house and land as his inheritance. This visit was part of that legal process. Strangely, they came the day after Deputy King had been there for a very different and secret reason. He didn't really want to return, but he was ordered to, so he decided to act like he was eager to go along with it.

The sheriff opened the front door casually—and was surprised that it wasn't locked. But what shocked him even more was the pile of men's clothing on the floor just inside. It looked like someone had taken them off and left them there. There were two hats, two coats, two vests, and two scarves. The clothes were still in good shape, just a little dusty. Brewer was just as surprised. As for King, his reaction wasn't mentioned. Feeling more alert now, the sheriff unlocked the door on the right side of the hallway, and the three men stepped into the room.

At first glance, it looked empty. But as their eyes adjusted to the dim light, they noticed something in the far corner. A man was crouched there. The strange way he was sitting made them freeze just after stepping inside. As they looked closer, the figure became clearer. The man was down on one knee, pushed deep into the corner. His shoulders were hunched high near his ears. His hands were raised in front of his face like claws, fingers spread and curled. His head was tilted back, and his pale face stared upward with wide, terrified eyes and a half-open mouth. He wasn't moving at all. He was dead. The only other thing in the room was a large knife on the floor near him—he had clearly dropped it.

In the thick dust on the floor, they could see footprints—some scattered near the door and along the wall. Another set of prints showed where the man had walked to the corner. The three men followed that trail. The sheriff reached down and touched one of the man's stiff arms. It felt as hard as metal. When he gently pulled it, the entire body rocked as one solid piece, like a statue.

Brewer's face turned pale. He stared at the twisted expression on the dead man's face. "Oh my God," he said. "It's Manton!"

"You're right," King said, trying to stay calm. "I knew him. He used to have longer hair and a beard, but this is him."

He could have said much more. He could've admitted: I knew who he was the second he challenged Rosser. I told Rosser and Sancher the truth before we went through with that awful plan. When Rosser ran out of the house with us, so shaken he left his coat behind and drove away in just his shirt sleeves, we already knew exactly who we had trapped. A murderer. A coward.

But King said none of that. Instead, he looked around the room, trying to figure out how Manton had died. It was clear he hadn't moved at all. He wasn't in a fighting position. His knife was on the ground. And the look on his face—it was clear he had died from fear. But what had scared him so badly? King didn't understand.

As he thought, his eyes drifted down to the dusty floor. What he saw made him freeze, even though it was the middle of the day and he wasn't alone. There, in the thick dust, leading straight from the door to the spot where Manton had died, were three sets of footprints. They were faint but clear—bare feet. The outer two were small, like children's. The middle one was a woman's. None of the prints turned back. They all pointed one way—toward the corner.

Brewer saw them too. He leaned forward, staring at the prints. He looked pale and shaken. "Look there!" he shouted, pointing at one of the woman's footprints. "The middle toe—it's gone. That was Gertrude!"

Gertrude was Mrs. Manton. She was also Brewer's sister.

The End

Thank You for Reading

Dear Reader,

We hope this timeless classic has sparked your imagination and enriched your literary journey. Now that you've turned the final page, we want to share a vision for the future of reading—one where every classic you've ever wanted to explore is at your fingertips, in a format that best suits your life.

We'd like to invite you to gain immediate, unlimited digital & audiobook access to hundreds of the most treasured literary classics ever written—along with the option to secure deluxe paperback, hardcover & box set editions at printing cost. Together, we can spark a new global literary renaissance alongside our small, independent publishing house called "The Library of Alexandria."

Thousands of years ago, the Library of Alexandria stood as a beacon of knowledge—until it was lost to history. We aim to reignite that spirit of preservation and discovery right now, in the modern age—only this time, it's accessible to all, in every language and every format.

Picture a world where every timeless classic, novel, poem, or philosophical treatise is not only available to read but also updated for today's readers—modernized, translated into any language or dialect, and ready to enjoy in any format you choose, whether that is in an eBook, audiobook, paperback, or deluxe hardcover & box set version a printing cost.

By joining our movement to rebuild the modern Library of Alexandria, you become part of an unprecedented mission to offer:

- **Unlimited Audiobook & eBook Access to the Greatest Classics of All Time**

  Instantly explore thousands of legendary works, from Plato and Shakespeare to Jane Austen and Leo Tolstoy. All are instantly ready to read or listen to, giving you a complete literary universe at your fingertips.

- **Paperback & Deluxe Editions at Printing Costs:**

  Purchase any title in a paperback, deluxe hardbound, or deluxe boxset edition at printing costs, shipped right to your doorstep. Curate your personal library of Alexandria with editions worthy of display— crafted to last, designed to captivate, and delivered straight to your door.

- **Modern translations for Contemporary Readers in all languages and dialects**

  Discover a vast selection of classics reimagined in clear, current language—no more struggling with outdated phrases or obscure references. Next to the original versions, we aim to offer translations in as many languages and dialects as possible.

  As we continue our translation efforts and add new languages, readers everywhere can connect with these works as if they were written today. By bridging linguistic divides, you're contributing to ensuring that these timeless stories become more meaningful, accessible, and inspiring for people across the globe.

- **Your Personal Library of Alexandria:**

  Over the months and years, you'll curate a unique physical archive of classics—each volume a testament to your taste, curiosity, and love of knowledge. It's not just about owning books—it's about curating a cultural legacy you'll cherish and pass down for generations to come.

- **Join a Global Literary Renaissance:**

  Your support fuels an ongoing mission: allowing us to reinvest in offering deluxe print editions (including special boxsets) at their true cost, broaden the range of available formats and translations, and extend the reach of these works to new audiences worldwide. By joining today, you're not just preserving a legacy of masterpieces; you set in motion a powerful wave of literary accessibility.

We are more than a publisher—we're a movement, and we can't do it alone. Your support lets us scale our mission, preserving and reimagining history's greatest works for tomorrow's readers.

Become a Torchbearer of knowledge.

Thank you for picking up this book and allowing us into your literary journey. As you turn the pages, know that you're part of something larger: a global effort to keep these stories alive, share their wisdom across borders and generations, and spark a true cultural revival for the modern era.

If this resonates with you—please consider taking the next step by visiting:

www.libraryofalexandria.com

With gratitude and a shared love of knowledge,

The Modern Library of Alexandria Team

Visit:

www.libraryofalexandria.com

Or scan the code below: